LOVELAND PUBLIC LIBRARY
000254937

W9-DEU-513

ANNA *in the* GARDEN

DIANE DAWSON HEARN

SILVER MOON PRESS
NEW YORK

First Silver Moon Press edition 1994

For information write:

Silver Moon Press
126 Fifth Avenue, Suite 803
New York, NY 10011

Printed in Hong Kong

10 9 8 7 6 5 4 3 2 1

Library of Congress Cataloging-in-Publication Data

Hearn, Diane Dawson
Anna in the garden / by Diane Dawson Hearn. – 1st ed.
p. cm.
Summary: Anna gets a package of seeds for her birthday in February, and she plants and cares for them and other flowers that grow in the garden throughout the year.
ISBN 1-881889-57-2 : $14.95
[1. Flowers–Fiction. 2. Gardening–Fiction.] I. Title
PZ7.H3455An 1994
[E]–dc20
93-442004
CIP
AC

To Betty Gallagher and her garden of children

February is bleak and cold, but Anna does not care. Today is her birthday. Among the many presents is a small package.

“What are these?” she asks, opening the package.

“Those are seeds,” says Anna’s mother. “Seeds for the spring garden.”

"But the garden is covered with snow," says Anna.

"We are not going to plant the seeds in the garden yet," Mother replies.

Mother brings some special pots and soil into the sun room. Together she and Anna plant the tiny seeds.

Spring is coming. The snow melts in the garden. Tulips and daffodils peek up through the wet earth. Crocuses are blooming.

Inside, warm and safe, the seeds are seedlings now.

Tulips and daffodils nod cheerfully in a spring breeze. Other plants turn green and sprout new leaves.

The whole garden is coming to life.

Now it is warm enough to plant the seedlings.

Anna picks a special place for them in the front of the garden.

When hot weather comes, weeds must be pulled.

Afterward, Anna waters all the flowers.

It takes a lot of work to grow a pretty garden.

So many flowers are blooming in the garden. Anna tries her best, but there are more than she can count.

The days are getting short as the leaves begin to turn.

Soon the growing season will be over.

Leaves are falling in the garden. Frost has killed the flowers Anna planted in the spring.

The other plants will stay and grow next year.

Winter is here.

Beneath the snow the plants and bulbs are sleeping. They are safe and still under their white blanket.

February comes again. Anna is a whole year older. Eagerly, she searches for a small package among her many presents.

She smiles when she finds it.

"Seeds," Anna says to her mother. "Seeds for the spring garden."

The Plants in Anna's Garden

Perennials

Once these plants take root in the garden, they come back year after year. Though the top leaves may turn brown and die, the roots below are dormant through the cold winter months, so the plants can grow again in the spring.

CONEFLOWER

LUPINE

BLACK-EYED SUSAN

HOSTA

DWARF ASTER

DWARF BLEEDING HEART
FOXGLOVE
DAISY
DAYLILY
ASTILBE
PHLOX
PEONY
POPPY
PRIMROSE
CAMPANULA

Bulbs

Bulbs are often planted in the fall, two to eight inches underground. In spring, they sprout up like magic. Many of them bloom year after year.

GRECIAN WINDFLOWER

CROCUS

SNOWDROP

LILY

HARD CYCLAMEN

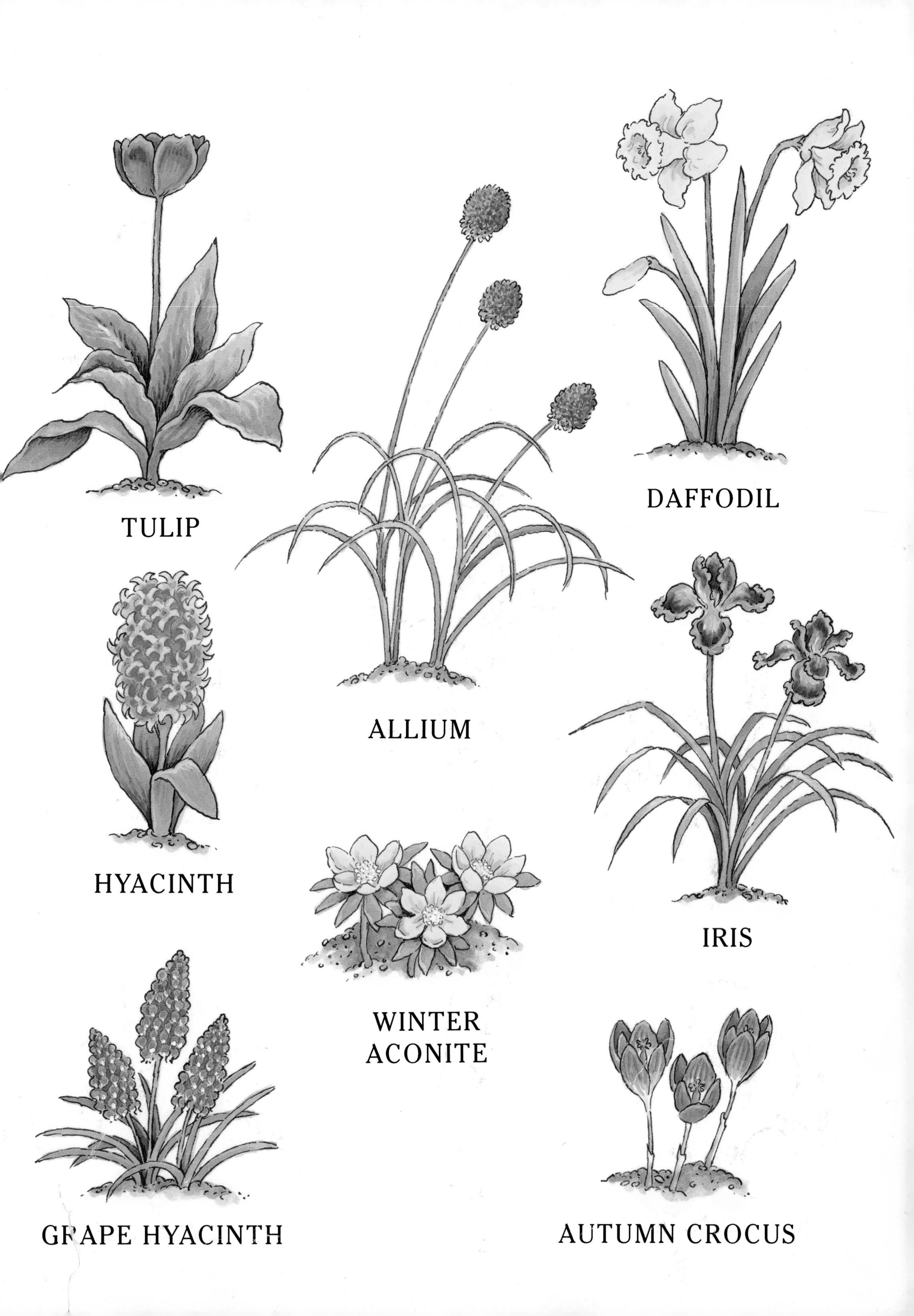
TULIP
ALLIUM
DAFFODIL
HYACINTH
IRIS
WINTER
ACONITE
GRAPE HYACINTH
AUTUMN CROCUS

Annuals

These are the flowers Anna grew from seeds. There are many kinds of annuals to grow in a garden. They cannot live through the cold winter, so new ones have to be planted each year.

ZINNIA

MARIGOLD

PANSY

IMPATIENS